Snow-White and the Dwarfs

AT LAST SHE CAME TO A LITTLE HUT

Page 13

SNOW-WHITE
AND
THE DWARFS

RETOLD BY

E. E. ELLSWORTH

BLACKIE & SON LIMITED
LONDON AND GLASGOW

BLACKIE & SON LIMITED
5 Fitzhardinge Street
London, W.1
Bishopbriggs, Glasgow

BLACKIE & SON (INDIA) LIMITED
103/5 Fort Street, Bombay

Printed in Great Britain by Blackie & Son, Ltd., Glasgow

CHAPTER ONE
The Wicked Queen

Long ago, in a far-off land, there lived a king and queen.

Both were very good and kind, and everybody loved them.

One day, when the queen was sitting sewing, she said to herself:

"I wish I had a little girl. I wish I had one with rosy cheeks, black hair, and a white skin. I should love a little girl like that."

Not long after, her wish came true. A dear little baby girl was born. She was so pretty. Her skin was snow-white, her cheeks were rosy, and her hair was black.

The king and queen were full of joy, and they called her Snow-White.

When little Snow-White was not very old, the good queen died. Everyone was very sad. Then the king began to look for another queen to be a mother to Snow-White.

At last he found one. She was very pretty, but she was not good. She liked everyone to think that she was pretty, and to say so too.

This queen had a magic looking-glass, and she used to talk to it. The glass could speak too.

Very often the queen said to the looking-glass:

" Looking-glass upon the wall,
Who is the prettiest one of all?"

Then the looking-glass always said:

"You are the prettiest one of all."

This always made the queen very glad. She did not like to think that anyone was as pretty as she.

As little Snow-White grew older, she grew prettier day by day. At last she was much prettier than the queen.

The queen did not know this for a long time, but one day she did find it out. She went to her looking-glass and said:

" Looking-glass upon the wall,
Who is the prettiest one of all?"

She thought that the glass would say that she was the prettiest. But the glass did not. It said:

"I will tell you what is true.
Snow-White is more fair than you."

When the queen heard this, she flew into a great rage. She made up her mind to get rid of little Snow-White. She wanted to be the prettiest again.

Then she called a man to her.

"Go away into the forest," she said. "Take

Snow-White away with you, and never let her come back. I do not wish ever to see her again."

So the man took Snow-White away. Far into the forest they went, but the man did not harm the little girl. He was sorry for her, and let her go when she begged him.

So the man went back without Snow-White, and the queen thought she had got rid of the little girl.

CHAPTER TWO

The Hut and the Seven Dwarfs

When Snow-White ran away from the man, she did not know where to go. She was afraid of the wild beasts, but they did not hurt her. So she ran on and on, for a very long time.

At last, tired out, she came to a hut.

"Oh! Here is a little house," she said. "I am

so tired. I hope they will let me come in and rest."

She tapped on the door, but nobody came. So she went in.

The hut was very small, but it was so clean and tidy. Snow-White was so glad to sit down.

There was a table with a clean cloth on it. Seven plates were on the table, with seven spoons, knives, forks, and mugs.

Snow-White had not eaten any food for a long

time, and felt very hungry. She did not know whose food it was, and she did not like to eat much. So she took a small bit of bread from each plate. Then she took a sip from each mug.

At one end of the room stood seven beds. They looked so clean and cosy. Snow-White longed to lie down on one, as she was very tired.

She got on the first bed, but she did not like

it.   She tried the next one, but that was no better.   One by one she tried them all, and the last one was the best.

Snow-White shut her eyes, and was soon fast asleep.

By and by the little men who lived in the hut came home.   They were dwarfs, and went away every day to dig for gold.   There were seven of them, and they were very kind little men.

Each dwarf had a little lamp of his own, and as soon as it was dark, they had to light them. The room looked so nice with seven lamps. They soon saw that

someone had been in the hut.

"Oh!" said one. "Who has sat on my chair?"

The next one said, "Who has eaten from my plate?"

The third one said, "Who has eaten some of my bread?"

The fourth one said, "Who has eaten some of my meat?"

The fifth one said, "Who has had my fork?"

The sixth one said,

"Who has cut with my knife?"

The seventh one said, "Who has drunk from my mug?"

Then one of them saw Snow-White fast asleep on a bed.

"Oh, look!" he said. "What a dear little girl! How sweet she is! We must not wake her up."

All the wee men came to look at Snow-White, and they all said that she was a dear little girl.

" She shall sleep in
that bed all night," said
the one whose bed it
was. So he got in bed with
one of the others and did
not wake the little girl.

The next day, when

Snow-White woke up, she saw the seven wee men. At first she felt afraid of them, but soon saw that they were kind.

"What is your name?" said one.

"My name is Snow-White," she said.

"Where do you come from?" said the wee men. "How did you get here?"

"The queen hates me," said Snow-White. "She sent me into the forest with a man. She told him to kill me, but he let me go. I ran for a long time, and at last I found this hut. I was very tired and I came in."

"Would you like to stay here?" said one of the wee men.

"Oh yes," cried Snow-White. "I should love to. I will cook for you, and sweep, and make the beds. I will do all there is to be done."

"Then you shall stay with us," said the kind dwarfs. "We will look after you, and keep you safe. You can cook for us, and then we can all go to look for gold."

How glad Snow-White felt! It was such a dear little hut. She loved making it look clean and tidy.

All day long she was busy. The birds sang sweet songs to her. The bees hummed and buzzed round the flowers, and the bunnies peeped out at her. Snow-White was very, very happy.

The wee men began to love her very much. They did not want the bad queen to hurt the little girl, so they said, "Do not open the door to anyone."

CHAPTER THREE

The Bad Queen Tries to Hurt Snow-White

For some time the queen did not speak to the magic glass. She was quite sure that Snow-White was dead. One day, however, she did talk to it again. She said:

"Looking-glass upon the wall,
Who is the prettiest one of all?"

Then the glass said:

"Snow-White in the forest
  green
Is the prettiest one, O
  queen."

The bad queen did not know what to do. She was so angry.

"I will go into the forest," she cried. "I will find Snow-White. She shall not be the prettiest one! I will be!"

Next day she set off into the forest. She made

herself look like a poor old woman, and she was sure Snow-White would not know her.

At last she came to the hut in the forest. She saw the little girl inside, and then she began to cry:

"Laces to sell. Laces to sell! Who'll buy my pretty laces?"

Snow-White peeped out of the window.

"Will you buy some laces?" asked the queen.

"No, thank you," said Snow-White.

"Oh, do buy some," begged the queen. "I am such a poor woman. Do buy some! Look! Here are some silk ones."

When Snow-White saw the silk laces, she opened the door. The queen came in and said, "Let me lace your clothes for you, my dear."

Snow-White did not know that the old woman was the bad queen, so she let her lace them up.

The queen began to lace her clothes. At first she did not hurt. Then she pulled the laces so tightly that poor Snow-White could not breathe.

She fell down on the floor of the hut. Away went the bad queen.

"Now I am the prettiest," she said to herself. "I have got rid of Snow-White."

Not long after, the wee men came home. When

they opened the door,
there was Snow-White on
the floor.

"Oh, dear! Whatever
is the matter?" they cried.
"Who has done this to
our little Snow-White?"

They were sure she was dead, but one of them saw the laces.

"Look!" he said. "Look at these laces. They are so tight that she cannot breathe. We must undo them, then she will be better."

Then one wee man cut the laces, and Snow-White began to feel better. She opened her eyes and sat up. How glad the little men were. They did not want Snow-White to be hurt.

"Tell us all about it," they said.

So Snow-White told them all about the old woman and the laces. Then the wee men said:

"That was not an old woman. It was the bad queen. You must not open the door to anyone at all. You must keep it shut and not let anyone come into the hut."

"I do not want the bad queen to hurt me again," said Snow-White. "If she comes here once more, I will not let her in."

So the next day, the little men went off to dig for gold. Snow-White stayed at home and cooked the meals.

Not long after the queen had been to the hut, she went to her looking-glass again, and said:

"Looking-glass upon the
    wall,
  Who is the prettiest one
    of all?"

The magic glass again said:

"Snow-White in the forest
    green,
  Is the prettiest one, O
    queen."

This made the queen more angry still, and she made up her mind to try again. She knew that Snow-White would not let her in, so she got some fresh clothes.

She put these on and made herself look like someone else. She felt quite sure that Snow-White would not know her.

Then she took a comb that was full of poison, and went off to the hut in the forest.

CHAPTER FOUR

The Comb

When the queen got to the little hut again, she saw that Snow-White was all alone. The wee men had gone away to work, and the little girl was busy.

The queen was glad. She knew that she could get into the hut if the dwarfs were not there. So she rapped on the door. Snow-White looked out of the window.

"You must go away," she said. "I do not want to buy anything!"

"Oh, please buy something," said the old woman. "Look at these nice combs. Here is such a pretty one. Do let me comb your hair for you."

So Snow-White opened the door again and let the queen in. She quite forgot that the dwarfs had told her not to do such a thing.

The bad queen took the comb that had the poison in it, and stuck it into Snow-White's hair.

" Oh," cried Snow-White. "Oh! Oh!"

Then she fell down, and the queen went off as fast as she could.

That night the wee men came home again, all ready for their supper. What a shock they had when they saw Snow-White on the floor.

" That bad queen has

been here again," they cried. "Why did Snow-White let her in? Look, here is a comb in her hair."

"Take it out," said one little dwarf. "Then our dear little Snow-White will be better."

So they took the comb out of her hair, and soon she sat up. When she felt better, she told them about the old woman.

"That old woman was the bad queen again."

said the dwarfs. "She is trying to hurt you, so do not open the door any more.'

"She did not look the same," said Snow-White. "I thought it was another old woman."

"You must take great care," said the wee men again. "Now, do not open the door to any-one."

CHAPTER FIVE

The Apple

When the queen got home, she did not go at first to her glass. She felt quite sure that the comb with the poison in it had killed Snow-White, so she waited.

After a week or so, she went to the glass. She stood in front and looked at herself, and then said:

"Looking-glass upon the wall,
Who is the prettiest one of all?"

Of course she quite thought the looking-glass would say to her: "You are the prettiest one."

But it did not. It said:

"Snow-White in the forest green,
Is the prettiest one, O queen."

The queen began to stamp with rage.

"She shall not be the prettiest one," she said. "I want to be the prettiest. I will not let her be better than I. No, I will not! I will get rid of her."

She made up her mind to try once more to kill Snow-White. At first she could not think of anything.

She sat in her room all by herself to think and think. At last she clapped her hands for joy. She had thought of something.

Soon she began to make something that looked just like a rosy apple. One side of it was green and the other half was red. In the rosy half the queen put some poison.

Then the queen got a basket and put some other apples inside it. She put the big rosy one on the top of the others, and it looked just like a pretty red apple.

Then she took some-
thing out of a bottle and
rubbed it on her face.
She got some clothes
she had not worn before,
and put them on.

When she was all
ready, she did not look
at all like a queen. She
looked just like an old
woman.

"I am quite sure that
Snow-White will not
know who I am," she
said to herself. "I will
give her this rosy apple,

if she will take it to eat."

So she put the basket on her arm, and went out. Soon she came to the forest where Snow-White lived with the wee men.

The queen went along very softly. She hoped to find the wee men away from home. When she got to the hut she looked in at the window. Once more she found Snow-White busy in the little hut.

"Good day, my dear," said the queen. "Will you buy my apples?"

"No, thank you," said Snow-White, peeping out of the open window.

"Oh, do buy a few," said the queen. "I am so poor and I do want to sell them."

"No, I cannot," said Snow-White. "I must not open the door or buy anything at all."

"Do not be afraid of me," said the bad queen.

"I am only a poor old woman. I would not hurt anyone."

Still Snow-White would not open the door.

Then the queen said:

"Well, if you will not buy my apples, I will give you one. Look at this rosy one. I am sure you would like it, and I will eat half to show you that it is good."

The queen then gave Snow-White the rosy half. She kept the green half, and then began to eat it.

When Snow-White saw the queen eating her half, she thought she could eat the other. So she began to eat it. She had only taken one bite, when she fell down.

"Ha! Ha!" cried the bad queen. "What a good thing! Now at last I am the prettiest one. I will go home and ask my magic glass."

So she went home as fast as she could. When

she got to her room, she
ran to her glass and
said:

"Looking-glass upon the
wall,
Who is the prettiest one
of all?"

Then the magic glass
said:

"You are the prettiest
one of all."

This made the bad
queen dance for joy. She
was so glad to hear the
glass say she was the

prettiest. So, every day for a long time she said to the magic glass:

"Looking-glass upon the wall,
Who is the prettiest one of all?"

Every time the glass told her that she was the prettiest. At last she did not ask it any more.

CHAPTER SIX

Snow-White and the Prince

When the little men came home they saw Snow-White on the floor. They looked to see if there were any laces to cut. They felt in her pretty black hair to see if the bad queen had put another comb there. They did not know what to do, for poor Snow-White did not move.

"Oh, dear," they cried sadly. "What shall we do? We cannot wake her up any more. What shall we do without our dear little Snow-White?"

They all felt that they must see her every day. She looked so pretty with her rosy cheeks. So they got a glass case, and put her inside. Then they could see her every day.

The little birds that used to sing to Snow-White were sad. So

were the little bunnies.
Everyone was sad
except the wicked queen.
So the wee men lived
alone, just as they did
before Snow-White came.
They had to cook their

own dinner, and sweep the floor, and make the beds. How they wished they had little Snow-White to help them.

A very long time after, a prince came riding by. He saw the little hut and the glass case. When he looked inside the case, and saw Snow-White, he stopped to watch her.

The prince said to the wee men:

"Do let me have this glass case. I have never

seen anyone so pretty."

"Oh, no," said the wee men. "We cannot let you have our Snow-White. We love her too much. We cannot part with her."

"Oh," said the prince. "I will pay you such a lot of money. Do let me take her away with me. I will take great care of her."

For a long time the little men said "No". They wanted her themselves. They loved her very much, and did not want her to be taken away.

"I will pay you as much money as you wish," said the prince again.

"We would not let our Snow-White go for all the gold in the world," they said.

At last the prince said:

"Give her to me, please. I cannot live without her."

Then the little dwarfs said:

"Yes, we will give her to you. We know you

will take great care of her."

The prince was so glad. He told his servants to pick up the case to carry it to his castle. Just as they were going away, one of them fell and almost dropped the case. This made the bit of apple fall out of Snow-White's mouth.

In a little time Snow-White opened her eyes.

"Where am I?" she said.

The prince was so glad

to see her alive, and he told her all about it. He said he would take her to his home where she would be quite safe. Snow-White was glad to go where the queen could not get her.

So she and the prince went far away to his land. Everyone loved her as much as the handsome prince.

The bad queen did not live very long. She broke her magic glass, and not long after she died.

And then Snow-White and the prince were married, and lived happily ever afterwards.

Jack-a-Dandy

Jack-a-Dandy

DOROTHY KING

Illustrated by Lilian Buchanan

BLACKIE & SON LIMITED

LONDON AND GLASGOW

BLACKIE & SON LIMITED
5 Fitzhardinge Street
London, W.1
17 Stanhope Street, Glasgow

BLACKIE & SON (INDIA) LIMITED
103/5 Fort Street, Bombay

Printed in Great Britain by Blackie & Son, Ltd., Glasgow

JACK-A-DANDY

CHAPTER I

How Jack-a-Dandy got his Name

JACK-A-DANDY! What a very funny name for any-one to have! Do you not think so? Well, first of all I must tell you that it was the name of a little man.

"He must have been a funny little man," you will say, "to have such an odd name." So he was. He lived long, long ago, all alone in a funny little house.

This house had white walls, a red roof, and a wee green door. It stood just at the far end of a town. Folk said it was so small that there was no room for any-one else when Jack went in! But then he was a very fat little man, so I think they must have been right!

Now there was an odd thing about Jack's house. Each room in it was almost full of—what do you think?

Why, *boxes!*

There were so many
boxes that there was no

room in the house for
more than one table, one
chair, and a small foot-
stool. So Jack had to

make his bed on the top of a big box.

I am sure you will not be able to think what so many boxes could hold. Gold, you will say, maybe, or silver? Not at all. Every box was full to the brim of fine things to wear.

There were rich coats and cloaks of silk and satin, hats with plumes in them, and many fine shoes. All these things were of as many shades as the rainbow—pink, blue, green, yellow.   No one in all that land had so many fine, rich things to wear as Jack-a-Dandy.

He had a fresh coat, cloak, and hat for every day in the year.   As for his shoes, no one was able to count how many pairs he had.

How fond he was of every fine dress in those boxes!   And how he loved to try on each in turn, before the glass, and to make him-self smart!

He used to put on a fresh

coat three times a day.
First he would wear a
green one, then a red, then
a blue. Now and then he
even wore two fine satin
coats at once!

When his work was
done, he would put on a
rich coat and cloak of silk,
and a hat with gold lace all
over it. Then he would
take a walk round the
town, just to show him-self
off.

He was so proud of him-
self, and of the fine things
he wore, that he would not

mix with the folk of the town. He used to strut

past them on his fat little legs, with his nose in the air. He was too full of pride to speak to those who lived near him.

"I am far too fine to mix with such poor folk," said he.

But you may be sure these folk did not like such silly, proud ways. "He is just a stuck-up little dandy," they said.

A dandy, you know, is some-one who is very smart, and very proud of what he wears.

And that was how this funny little man got the name of Jack-a-Dandy.

CHAPTER II

Plum Cake and Sugar Candy

Now there was something else that Jack-a-Dandy loved as well as fine things to wear. That some-thing else was sweet things to eat. He was just as fond of cakes and sweets as any boy or girl.

He liked every kind of cake and every kind of sweet, no matter what it was. But the kind of cake he liked best of all was *plum cake.* And there was no sweet he liked so much as *sugar candy.*

But there was one thing that made Jack very sad. I will tell you what it was. In the town where he lived, there was no plum cake or sugar candy to be had. There was no shop that sold even a tiny bit of plum cake or a single stick of candy.

You may be sure that the boys and girls of the town found this very hard when they had a penny to spend.

Jack feels very sad

Still, some-times they had cake and candy made for them at home. But Jack did not know how to make such things. So it was not often that he was able to have the treat he liked best.

One day Jack-a-Dandy set off from his house for a walk. The road he took ran by a little wood. Very soon, under the trees of the wood, he saw a tiny white house.

"Why, who can live there?" said Jack to him-self. "I have never seen that house before."

He went up to the door. There was a big green board with these words upon it:

PLUM CAKE
AND
SUGAR CANDY
SOLD HERE

Jack gave a great jump for joy. Then he took a peep in the window. It was set out like the window of a shop. And it was full of piles and piles of

plum cake and rows and
rows of sugar candy!

Before you could wink

an eye, Jack was in that
funny little shop. There
he found an ugly old dame
in a red cloak.

"What can I get for you, sir?" said she.

"I want six pounds of plum cake, and ten sticks of sugar candy!" said Jack.

The old dame put the cake and the candy into a big bag, and Jack paid for them. Then he set off for home again, as fast as he could go.

"How glad I am," said he to him-self, "that at last I have found a cake-and-candy shop so near home! Now I can have these nice things as often as I like!"

What a feast Jack had that night! He had never had any cake or candy in all his life that was half so good as this.

Soon he began to go two or three times a week to the wee shop in the wood. The old dame came to know him very well, and took care to save all her cake and candy for him.

The boys and girls of the town found out the shop too. But there was never any cake or candy for them. Jack-a-Dandy used to buy every bit of it! They said this was not fair. But then Jack did not stop to think of any-one else, when plum cake and sugar candy were to be had.

He grew to love cake and candy more and more every day. He was soon so fond of these sweet things that the boys and girls made a little song about him.

This was the way they used to tease him. When he took a walk round the town, they would join hands and dance behind him in a

row; and then they would
sing:

"*Handy, pandy, Jack-a-Dandy
Loves plum cake and sugar
candy*".

CHAPTER III

How he spoilt his New Coat

One day Jack-a-Dandy put on a grand new dress that he had never worn before. The coat and hat were of blue satin and gold lace, and the coat was trimmed with fine white fur.

Jack was going out for the day, to visit a great lord whom he knew. So he had made up his mind to be very, very smart.

He went down the street of the town with his nose high in the air. How funny he was, with his little fat body in that gay dress, and his little short legs!

The boys and girls left their play to watch him go by. At last they joined hands, and came after him with a hop, skip, and a jump; and then they sang:

"Handy, pandy, Jack-a-Dandy
Loves plum cake and sugar
candy".

But Jack's mind was so full of his fine dress, and of

what a gay sight he was, that he did not care a bit. He would not even look at them.

By and by he left the town, and came to a road that led to the lord's castle. On one side of this road there was a big pond full of muddy water.

Jack did not look at the pond as he went by. But all at once he heard some-one call in a voice full of fear:

"Help! help! or I shall sink!"

Jack ran up at once. And there, in the middle of the pond, was a poor old dame, up to her neck in the water.

"Help! help! or I shall sink!" she cried again as Jack came near.

And now he did not stop to think of his new coat. With a jump and a splash, he was in the pond too. Oh, how cold and dirty that horrid water was! But he took fast hold of the dame, and was soon able to drag her to the bank.

At last they were both on dry land again. The old dame shook with fear and

cold. Her cloak, too, was wet and muddy.

But Jack-a-Dandy was

not one bit like a dandy now! Where was the lovely satin coat he had put on with such pride an hour ago? He still wore it, to be sure, but oh, what a sight it was!

It was wet from neck to hem, and you could not have told what shade it had once been. All over it, there were marks of nasty green slime and dark brown mud. It could never be made nice again. His fine new coat was spoilt for ever.

CHAPTER IV

The Wish

"Oh, dear! What a mess I am in!" cried poor Jack. Then he looked at the old dame. Who was it, do you think? Why, the old woman who sold plum cake and sugar candy, at the wee shop in the wood!

"Dear me," said she, "I am so sorry, for I am to blame for all this. What can I do to make up to you for the loss of your fine new coat?"

"I must go home at once," said Jack. "I shall not be able to go to my lord's grand castle in this state. Good-bye, dame."

"Wait a little," said the dame, "I must do something for you, as you have done so much for me.

"Oh, I know what I will do! I will give you a wish!"

"A wish!" cried Jack.

"Yes. Some folk call me a witch," went on the old

dame with a smile, "but, any-how, I never harm them; and, to those who

do me a good turn, I can give a wish that will come true. Now, what is there that you wish for? Tell me, and you shall have it, what-ever it may be."

It took Jack a long time to think this over. What should he wish for? More fine things to wear? A grand new house, and a great deal of money? He was just about to speak, when the old dame began to sing in a soft voice:

"Handy, pandy, Jack-a-Dandy
Loves plum cake and sugar
candy".

"Why, to be sure I do," cried Jack, "better than any-thing else in the world!

Plum cake and sugar candy for ever and ever! I will not have any-thing else to eat, as long as I live! For I am sure I shall never get tired of them!"

"Very well," said the old dame with a smile, "we shall see!"

———

CHAPTER V

Too much of a Good Thing

When Jack got home, he found he was wet to the skin, and very, very cold.

"I will have a bowl of nice, hot bread-and-milk,"

said he, "and then I will go to bed."

He soon got the bread-and-milk ready. But, when

he sat down to eat it, what do you think took place? Why, there was no bread-and-milk to be seen any-where! On his plate, in place of the bowl, was a large, round plum cake and a long stick of sugar candy!

What a shock Jack got at first! Then he began to think of his wish: " Plum cake and sugar candy, for ever and ever".

"Oh, well," said he, " I don't mind." And he ate up the cake and candy, and went off to bed. But I think he was sorry that there was no bread-and-milk for him that night.

Every day after that the same thing took place. Every-thing he got ready to eat would change to cake and candy before his eyes.

If he went to buy meat, or bread, or fish, in the town, he found it was cake and candy, by the time he got home.

At first he liked this very much. You see, he was so very fond of plum cake and sugar candy. It did not seem, at first, as if he could ever have too much of such nice things.

But, by and by, he began to get just a wee bit tired of them. Plum cake and

sugar candy for breakfast!
Plum cake and sugar candy
for dinner! Plum cake and
sugar candy for supper!
The sight of nice food made
him quite sad, for he knew
that, when he tried to taste
it, it would turn to plum
cake and sugar candy.

At last he began to feel
sick at the sight of cake
and candy. Then he grew
to hate the taste of them.

He never went near the
wee shop in the wood now.
He had no need, and no
wish to do so. And oh!

how cross he grew, when the boys and girls used to dance at his heels and sing:

"Handy, pandy, Jack-a-Dandy
Loves plum cake and sugar
candy".

"Oh, now I know that one can have too much of a good thing!" said Jack.

CHAPTER VI

"Just for a Change"

At last, Jack made up his mind to go and see the old witch at the wee shop in the wood.

"I will ask her to take back the wish she gave me," said he. "For, oh, how tired I am of plum cake and sugar candy! I don't think I ever want to taste them again!"

The very look of the old witch's shop-window made

The wee shop in the wood

him feel quite ill.   He found her in the shop, and told her all his tale.

"Oh, please, *please,* dame, take back the wish!"   he said at last.

But the old witch only gave a smile.

"I cannot take your wish back," said she, "but, if you like, I can change it for you a little.

"Now, Jack-a-Dandy, I know you love fine things to wear as much as you once loved cake and candy. You love to put on a fine coat every day, don't you?

"Well, just for a change, every day that you wear a coat that is old, or dirty, or torn, you may have to eat what-ever you wish. But, on the days that you choose to wear a fine coat, then you will have only cake and candy to eat. And this is all that I am able to do for you."

CHAPTER VII

Jack in a Fix

What do you think was the first thing Jack did when he got home again?

He went to one of his boxes, and took out a dirty old coat. It was so old that it was nearly worn to rags. At any other time, the sight of such a poor thing to wear would have made Jack turn up his nose.

But now he put it on

with joy. And then he sat
down to a big plate full of
plain bread-and-butter! He

ate it all, and did not leave
one slice! And oh, how
good it tasted, after so
many sweet foods!

So now, for some time, Jack wore the oldest and most shabby coats he could find. He had every-thing to eat that he could wish for. But he would not touch one thing that was sweet. You see, he did not wish even to think of cake or candy for a long time.

All this while he kept in the house, and would not go out at all. He did not want the folk of the town to see him in his shabby coats.

But, one fine day, he

grew tired of all this, and did not stop to think of the old witch's words. He put on a rich red silk coat, and a cloak of green satin. Then he set off to walk round the town with his nose in the air, as of old.

But, oh dear! When he got home he found only plum cake and sugar candy to eat for the rest of the day! How he hated them!

He would not touch his supper at all that night.

And now Jack was in a fix. He loved fine things

to wear, but, when-ever he
wore them, he must have
only cake and candy to

eat. At the same time, if
he wished to eat any-thing
else, he had to wear dirty

old coats that were all in rags.

And he hated shabby things to wear, as much as he now hated plum cake and sugar candy.

For he was such a dandy, you know!

CHAPTER VIII

"New Coats for Old"

At last, one day, a queer old man came to the town where Jack lived. He wore a long coat that was half black and half yellow, and on his back was a heavy pack.

He had a great white beard that came down to his knees. His eyes were bright blue and very merry.

Down the street he went, and on his way he cried out: "New coats for old! New coats for old! Bring out your old coats, and you shall have new ones!"

A crowd came round him, and he began to open his big pack. It was full of fine new silk coats of every sort and shade.

In great joy, the folk of the town gave up all their old coats, and got new ones in place of them. How smart every-one was!

At last some-one said: "Where is Jack-a-Dandy? Why does he not come out of his house, to get his share of such fine things?"

"Jack-a-Dandy!" said the queer old man, "I will go and find him." And away he went to Jack's house, crying: "New coats for old!"

But when Jack heard him, and saw the fine things in his pack, he said sadly:

"I do not want any more new coats. I shall never wear such smart things again."

And he felt so sad that he told the old man all his story.

"I never mean to taste plum cake or sugar candy again all my life long," said he. "So that means that I must wear shabby coats for the rest of my life. But, oh dear! How sorry I am!"

"You have been very silly and vain and greedy," said the old man, "to think

so much of fine things to wear and sweet things to eat. That old witch at the wee shop in the wood has been able to play a fine trick on you. But I think I can help you, after all."

CHAPTER IX

An Odd Coat

With these words, the old man took from his pack the oddest coat that Jack had ever seen.

One half of it was of rich pink satin, and silver cloth, and lace. And the other half was just a mass of dirty old rags!

It was such an odd coat that Jack could only stand and stare at it. But the old man held it up with a gay laugh.

"I will give you this to wear," said he. "You see, it is new as well as old, and smart as well as shabby. So it is bound to be the right thing for you! And, every day that you put it on, you may eat what-ever you please."

"But must I wear it always?" cried Jack, for he began to think that such a coat was far worse than one that was all rags. How the folk of the town would laugh at him when he wore it!

"You must wear this coat and no other for a year and a day," said the old man. "And, all that time, you must go among the good folk of this town. But you must not show your-self proud or vain. You are no better and no worse than they, you know. One half of you will be a dandy, but the other half

will be just a ragged Jack.
"If you do this for a year
and a day, you will be able to

wear what you like, and eat
what you wish, after that.
"Yes! And I think you

will even be able to like plum cake and sugar candy once again."

CHAPTER X

Happy at Last

When the old man had gone, and left the odd coat behind him, Jack made up his mind that he would wear it. You see, he *did* so wish to become like other folk once more!

So he put on the coat, and went out in the town.

But, this time, he did not strut about with his nose in the air. He was not quite a dandy, for half of him was in rags. So he had no cause to be proud.

The folk stood still to stare at him, and at first they began to laugh. But Jack tried not to mind their smiles. He made up his mind to do as the old man had told him.

So he stood to speak with one or two folk, and did his best to be kind and gay.

At last he told them all
his story, and how silly and
greedy he had been. "But

I mean to change now,"
said he.

And he kept his word.

Every day, after that, he went out in the town in that odd coat. He did not show any pride now, and soon he did not think of his looks at all. His mind was full of other things, and of how he could make other folks happy.

By and by, every-one grew to love him. And, when the year and the day had gone by, Jack made a grand dinner for all the folk of the town. You may be sure that every-one went to it.

Jack wore a nice new coat, but he was not a bit proud of it. He was glad to put off his rags, but he had put off his pride as well, you see.

Now, at the dinner, an odd thing took place. On the table, for the sake of the boys and girls, were plum cake and sugar candy. To please them all, Jack took a wee taste himself. And then he found that the cake and candy were nicer than ever before! But, this time, he would not take too much of them.

"As much as one can eat
is as good as a feast!" said
Jack-a-Dandy.

THE TEN LITTLE FISHES

THE TEN
LITTLE FISHES

JOAN WOOLDRIDGE

Illustrated by Anne Linton

BLACKIE: LONDON & GLASGOW

Blackie & Son Ltd., 5 Fitzhardinge Street, London, W.1
17 Stanhope Street, Glasgow
Blackie & Son (India) Ltd., Bombay

Printed in Great Britain by Blackie & Son, Ltd., Glasgow

CONTENTS

MR. BIGGS MAKES A FISH-POND

Mr. and Mrs. Biggs lived in a little red brick house. They had a garden with a brown wooden fence, and all round the edge of the garden there was a border with poppies, lupins, pinks, daisies and many other gay flowers. In the middle was a soft green lawn like a carpet where Mary, their little girl, used to play. An oak tree grew in one corner, and Mary had a swing hanging from the branches.

One day Mr. Biggs said, 'I am going to make a fine fish-pond in the garden. It shall be in the centre of the lawn. The bottom and sides shall be paved with blue tiles, and I will put sea-shells round the edge, lovely coloured sea-shells, to make it look pretty.'

Mrs. Biggs and Mary were very happy. When the new pond was ready they went by bus into the town to choose some fish to swim in it. Mary had had some money for her birthday which was a week ago, and so they went straight to the shop and asked Mrs. Brown, the kind person in the pet shop, how many fishes the money would buy.

You can guess how pleased Mary was when she heard that they could have ten.

What fun she had choosing them!

Four were gold, two were gold and black, three were pink and grey and one was the most beautiful of all, a gleaming silver with black stripes.

Mrs. Brown said that her husband would bring the fish out to Mary's house in his van after the shop was shut. She put them into a big glass tank full of water until her husband was ready.

Sure enough, at six o'clock that evening the fish arrived at Mrs. Biggs's house.

The pond was looking lovely by now, as Mr. Biggs had spent the afternoon planting water-lilies in it. He took the tank of fish from Mr. Brown's hands, and very gently carried it to the pond and tipped them in. Then Mr. Biggs, Mrs. Biggs and Mary all stood round the pond and said how much they liked having their very own fishes swimming in the water in their very own garden.

THE MISSING FISHES

What do you think Mary did first thing the next morning? She put on her clothes in a hurry, went outside and ran over the lawn to see her fishes. There they were swimming happily in the early morning sunshine. She began to count. 'One, two, three, four, five, six, seven, eight, nine.' Yes, nine. That was all. 'Perhaps one is hiding underneath a water-lily,' she thought, so she peeped underneath each one. But there wasn't a fish under the water-lilies. There were still only nine.

She ran back into the house to tell Mr. and Mrs. Biggs. They came hurrying out to count too, but still there were only nine. Where could that fish be?

'Never mind, Mary,' said Mr. Biggs, 'don't be sad, you still have all the others.' So Mary played all day long in the garden and in the evening she went upstairs to bed.

Next morning she woke up as soon as it was light, dressed quickly and tip-toed softly downstairs and into the garden. She went straight to the pond and started to count. 'One, two, three, four, five, six, seven, eight.'

Yes, eight. That was all.
Quickly she fetched her
mother and father, but
they could only count
eight too.

The next night the same thing happened. In the morning Mary counted the fishes. 'One, two, three, four, five, six, seven.' Yes, seven. That was all. Whatever could be the matter?

'Well, Mary,' said her mother, 'we must all watch and listen hard to see what happens. Father and I always go to bed late, so we should hear if anyone came to the pond in the evening. You must get up very early in the mornings to watch then. We can't lose all the pretty fish.'

That evening Mr. and Mrs. Biggs listened hard until bed-time, but all was quiet and still.

MARY WATCHES IN THE EARLY MORNING

The next morning Mary was awake early. She dressed herself and went downstairs and into the garden. The early morning sun was shining on the dewy grass and all the birds were singing round her.

She ran across the

grass and was soon standing at the sea-shell border of the pond.

Looking into the clear water she began to count her fishes.

'One, two, three, four, five, six, seven.' Yes, seven. Still seven. That was a good thing, the same number as yesterday.

'I will fetch a deck-chair from the garden shed,' said Mary, 'then I can sit in the corner just behind the oak tree and peep out to see if anyone comes. No one will be able to see me there, but I shall be able to see the pond.'

Presently Mary felt tired; she had got up so early. Her head started to nod and a terrible thing happened, she fell asleep. When she woke up, it was much later; the sun was high and the dew dry on the grass.

'Perhaps I had better make sure that everything is as it should be,' she thought to herself. So she walked across the grass again very softly and started to count. 'One,

two, three, four, five, six.'
Yes, six. That was all.
Someone had stolen a
fish while she had been
asleep.

Her mother and father
were sad for her when
she told them what had
happened. 'You must
watch more carefully
than that,' they said.

Next morning too Mary
was out in the garden
early. The air was very
hot and heavy, and as
Mary sat in her deck-

chair she thought that it was not nearly as nice as yesterday. Black clouds gathered in the sky and all the birds stopped singing. Then far away she heard a rumbling noise. Soon it grew louder, lightning flashed across the sky and large spots of rain began to fall. 'Oh, dear!' said Mary, 'A thunderstorm! I must go inside.'

Great hail-stones beat upon the roof of the house

and Mary could hear the thunder crashing. 'Someone is having a great storm,' she said.

At last it was all over. Mary tip-toed out into the garden again. She went straight to the fish-pond and started to count. 'One, two, three, four, five.' Yes, five. That was all.

Her mother and father tried to comfort Mary.

'It will not be a thunderstorm again tomorrow,'

said Mr. Biggs, 'so you
will be sure to see what
happens.'

Mary slept well that
night. It had seemed such
a long day and she was so
tired. But she was up
early again the next
morning and was soon

out in the garden. Then just as she sat down in her deck-chair behind the oak tree she heard a most peculiar noise. What could it be? Mary gazed across the lawn and saw a mother hedgehog and her two small baby hedge-hogs out looking for food. They had been out nearly all night (hedgehogs stay awake at night and sleep in the day), and now were on their way home. For a moment they stopped to eat a juicy slug and then the little ones followed their mother right over the lawn to the garden gate.

Mary had never seen a baby hedgehog before. She was so excited that she tip-toed after them. There was a hole underneath the gate big enough for the hedgehogs to squeeze through, but Mary, of course, had to walk out of the gate.

Down the lane went the strange little line. Mother

Hedgehog first, the two babies next and last of all Mary. A thick hedge grew along the sides of the lane. Suddenly the mother hedgehog turned to go into it and so did the

little ones. Mary held her breath so that they should not hear her, and as she looked she saw their nest tucked well back into the hedgerow. 'Oh, I'm so glad I followed you,' she thought, 'I've found where you live and I won't ever tell anyone. Now I must

go back to my fish-pond
to look at my fishes and
see if they are all right.'

She went back along the
lane and through the gar-
den gate. Everything was
quiet and still and Mary
was sure that nothing
could have happened in
such a short time.

At the pond she stopped
and looked. There was a
ripple on the waters.
Mary started to count.
'One, two, three, four.'
Yes, four. That was all.

MRS. BIGGS GETS UP EARLY

When Mary told her mother and father they were very sad to think that another fish was lost. Mrs. Biggs said, 'If we go on losing the fish so quickly there will soon be not one left. I will get up early tomorrow morning with you myself and then one of us will certainly see what happens.'

Early the next morning Mary put two deck-chairs behind the big oak tree in the corner—one for her mother and one for herself. Mary was glad to have someone to watch with her. They both kept very still, they wanted so much to find out what happened to the fish.

There was hardly a sound to be heard in the garden. The time seemed very long. Mary thought, 'My mother is watching this morning so I will shut my eyes for a few minutes I feel so sleepy.'

Her mother was tired too. She had had a busy day yesterday. 'Mary is watching,' she said to herself. Soon her head began to nod and she was asleep too.

As the church clock struck seven, Mrs. Biggs woke up with a start. She looked at her little girl and saw that Mary was fast asleep. Mrs. Biggs leaped out of the deck-chair and ran to the pond. She started to count. 'One, two, three.' Yes, three. That was all.

'Tomorrow morning we really must stay awake,' said Mrs. Biggs. 'We do not want to lose any more fish. I will watch you to see that you do not go to sleep and you must watch me.'

Next morning they were both up early. The time seemed longer than ever. At last Mrs. Biggs could bear it no more. 'Mary,' she said, 'I am going indoors to make some tea. I feel so sleepy, but that will keep us awake.'

'That is a good idea,' said Mary. 'I will come and help you and we shall be back here very soon.'

Mary and her mother went into the house. In five minutes time they came out into the garden again with the tea.

As they were shutting the door, Mary clutched her mother's arm. There was a strange noise, grow-

ing softer and softer into the distance. It sounded as if something with great wings, slowly beating, was flying through the air.

There was no sound in the garden. The poppies

and lupins in the border looked quite undisturbed. Mary had a dreadful feeling though that something was wrong. So she ran quickly to the pond and started to count. 'One, two.' Yes, two. That was all. 'Oh, Mother, Mother!' she cried. 'We have only two fishes left now. Soon there will be none left at all.'

V

THE STRANGE VISITOR IS FOUND OUT

When Mr. Biggs came down to breakfast that morning he said, 'Well, have you caught whoever it is who is taking our fish? With both of you watching I expect it was easy.'

Mary looked sadly at Mrs. Biggs, and Mrs.

Biggs looked sadly at Mary. Together they told Mary's father what had happened.

'Well, just think of that!' he said. 'Two of you keeping guard and still we do not know who comes. There is only one thing to be done. To-morrow morning I will get up early with you my-self and then we really will see what happens.'

So next morning they were all up early.

'I will make a thermos flask of tea to take out with us,' said Mrs. Biggs, 'and then we shall none of us have to come inside the house for anything.'

43

Soon they were all ready.

Mary went first through the kitchen to the backdoor. She turned the handle and peeped out into the garden. Everything smelt fresh and dewy and the flowers were bright in the early morning sunshine.

Mary looked towards the pond and nearly cried out in amazement. Quickly she stopped and put her finger on her lips, then turned to her mother and father who were just behind, and pointed excitedly. The three of them stood quite still in astonishment and gazed across the lawn at the pond.

There sitting by the sea-shell border was a large bird. Much bigger than any of the birds who usually came to the garden. It had grey wings with dark tips and a long thin head. It was gazing

at the water with two
clear blue eyes.

Then quick as lightning

it swooped with its beak and Mary and her mother and father all gave a great big shout as it swallowed a fish in one neat gulp.

Away flew the bird frightened by the terrific noise and soon it was quite out of sight.

Mary went sadly to the pond and counted. 'One.' Yes, one. That was all. The beautiful silver fish with the black stripes was the only one left.

Mr. Biggs shook his head. 'Well, well, well,' he said thoughtfully, 'whoever would have thought that a *heron* was making our fish disappear? We cannot really blame him because herons live on fish and frogs. But he must not do it again and catch our very last one. I must think hard until I have a plan.'

MR. BIGGS HAS A WONDERFUL
PLAN

In the morning Mr. Biggs thought very hard at breakfast-time. Usually he would read the newspaper while he ate his bacon and eggs, but to-day he just thought and thought.

At last he smiled. 'I have a good idea,' he said,

'and Mary, you shall help me. Bring your tape-measure, a paper and a pencil, and we will go out to the pond together.'

Mary finished her breakfast quickly, and out they went to the garden.

'Now,' said her father, 'I am going to see exactly how long and how wide the pond is, and you shall write it down for me on the piece of paper.'

When this was done,

Mary's father said, 'Now I am going to catch the bus into town to buy the things that I shall need for my plan. You may come too if you like and help me carry them.'

So they said 'Goodbye' to Mrs. Biggs, and off they went.

When they reached the town, they went to the timber yard first of all. Mr. Biggs bought two long thin pieces of wood exactly as long as the pond, and two more pieces exactly as wide as the pond. They paid the timber yard man and thanked him. 'Please let me carry the wood,' said

Mary, and she held it very carefully so as not to poke it into anyone's face.

Then they went along to the hardware shop.

At the hardware shop Mr. Biggs bought a large strip of thin wire-netting, and the man who served them rolled it up neatly for Mr. Biggs to carry home. Then they bought some small nails and some tacks.

All the shopping was done now, and so they

caught the next bus home again.

That afternoon Mr. Biggs was very busy. Can you guess what he was doing?

Yes, he was making a cover of wire-netting to go right over the top of the fish-pond. First he made a frame with the four pieces of wood. He nailed them firmly together at the corners. Then he spread the wire-netting across from one

side to the other and
nailed it into place.

When it was ready, Mary and Mr. Biggs carried it to the pond, and laid it over the top of the water. They hid the wooden frame under the sea-shell border.

Early the next morning Mr. and Mrs. Biggs and Mary all waited at the kitchen window to see if the heron would come.

Soon they heard the flapping of its wings and saw it fly to the edge of the pond. But what was this? The heron looked hard at the netting. He saw the silver fish and tried to catch it with his long beak. But he could not. He tried again and again but it was of no use.

Then Mary and her mother and father all clapped their hands for joy and shouted, and the heron flew away for the last time.

MARY BUYS SOME NEW FISHES

'Well, I don't think the heron will come to our fish-pond again,' said Mr. Biggs.

'No,' said Mary, 'but we have only one fish left in it now.'

'Don't be sad, Mary,' said her mother. 'We will think of a way to get you

some more. The fishes
cost a shilling, didn't they?
And a shilling is two sixpences. Why don't you
sell some flowers from
your own piece of garden?
Many people would be
very glad to pay sixpence
for a pretty bunch of
flowers.'

'What a good idea!'
said Mary, and that morn-
ing after breakfast she
went into the garden and
picked six bunches of
flowers. She made the

bunches look as pretty as she could, and in the middle of each she put a rose-bud to make the bunch smell nice. Then she tied them with green raffia.

'I will make a notice now,' she said. She found a board, and on it she printed in large letters,

'FLOWERS FOR SALE. SIXPENCE A BUNCH.'

Then she put the flowers in a big bowl of

water and stood them on
a table with the notice in
the garden where every-
one could see.

At last she had sold
them all.

'Well done, Mary,' said her mother. 'Now you have six sixpences. Two sixpences make a shilling, so six sixpences make three shillings and three shillings will buy three beautiful fishes. And because you have worked so hard, Father and I will give you twelve more sixpences, then you will have ten little fishes again.'

It was a great day when Mary and her mother went into the town to the

pet shop. They chose
fishes of just the same
colours as the ones they
had lost.

That evening when the

fish were all swimming happily in the water in Mr. Biggs's garden, Mary and her mother and father stood round the pond and looked at them lovingly.

'You can swim as happily as you like,' said Mary. 'The heron will never catch you now.'

And he never, never did.